D1383337

The Origin of
Day and
Night

Published by Inhabit Media Inc.
www.inhabitmedia.com

Inhabit Media Inc. (Iqaluit) P.O. Box 11125, Iqaluit, Nunavut, X0A 1H0
(Toronto) 191 Eglinton Avenue East, Suite 310, Toronto, Ontario, M4P 1K1

Design and layout copyright © 2018 Inhabit Media Inc.
Text copyright © 2018 Paula Ikuutaq Rumbolt
Illustrations by Lenny Lishchenko © 2018 Inhabit Media Inc.

Editors: Neil Christopher, Kelly Ward, and Kathleen Keenan
Art director: Danny Christopher

This project was made possible in part by the Government of Canada.

We acknowledge the support of the Canada Council for the Arts for our publishing program.

Library and Archives Canada Cataloguing in Publication

Ikuutaq Rumbolt, Paula, 1990-, author
        The origin of day and night / by Paula Ikuutaq
Rumbolt ; illustrations by Lenny Lishchenko.

ISBN 978-1-77227-180-5 (hardcover)

        I. Lishchenko, Lenny, illustrator II. Title.

PS8617.K89O75 2018   jC813'.6   C2018-904509-4

Printed in Canada

The Origin of Day and Night

by Paula Ikuutaq Rumbolt

illustrated by Lenny Lishchenko

INHABIT
MEDIA

At the very beginning of time, there was no light on earth. Darkness surrounded everything. Only nocturnal animals, those who could see in the dark, could easily hunt for food.

Tiri, the Arctic fox, was lucky enough to have a pair of eyes that could see in the dark. He could hunt animals while they were sleeping and steal from the secret places where humans hid their food.

This was also a time of magic words, when things that were spoken aloud could become real. Tiri loved the darkness so much that he called out, "*Taaq, taaq, taaq!* Darkness, darkness, darkness!" And so it remained dark.

In the darkness, Tiri hunted for little animals to eat. Like the lemming he had been sniffing out for hours. Prancing around on the soft snow as quietly as he could, Tiri found the lemming's home and jumped as high as he could. He dove head-first into the fluffy snow right above the little burrow where the lemming was sleeping. He came out with the lemming in his mouth.

But someone else had heard Tiri calling out—Ukaliq, the Arctic hare.
Though she did not have the special eyes that could see in the dark, she
could hear the fox. She wondered what would happen if she called
out the word for day, so she said, "*Ubluq, ubluq, ubluq!* Day, day,
day!" Slowly, the world became bright.

Tiri's vision began to dull. He looked around as
quickly as he could and spotted Ukaliq.

Tiri yelled, "What did you do? I can't
see anything."

The fox and the hare weren't the fondest of friends. Tiri tried hunting Ukaliq from time to time, because he knew that she couldn't see him. She ran away whenever she heard him or felt his presence.

"I would like to find my own food in the brightness. I cannot see in the dark," Ukaliq told him, munching on some moss.

"I'm not done eating yet. That lemming was too small, and I am still hungry," Tiri said. He ran about, repeating, "Taaq, taaq, taaq!" The darkness came back.

Ukaliq perked up her ears and twisted them toward the noise the fox was making.

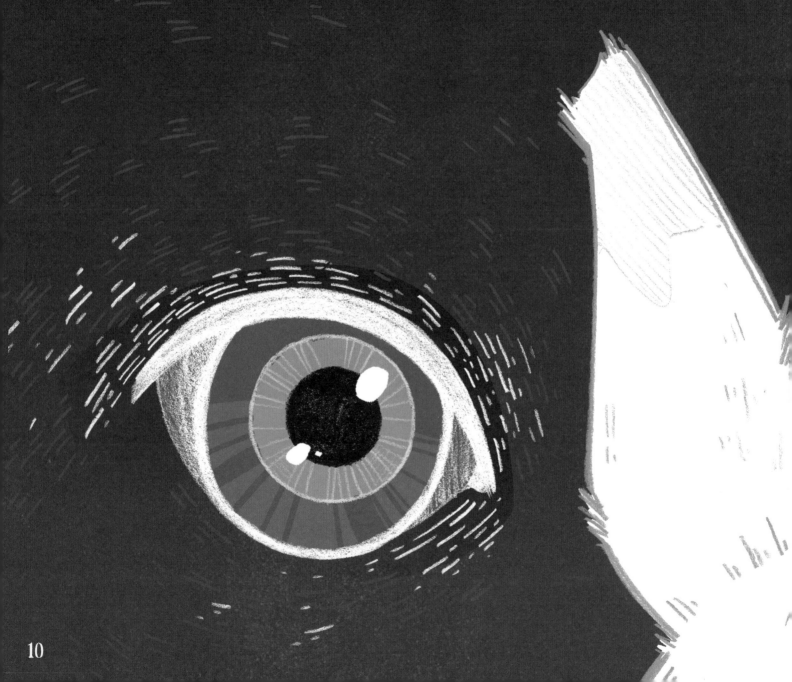

Tiri was about to chase the hare, but as he moved toward her, he caught the scent of another animal. He could tell by the smell that this animal was much tastier than a hare or even a lemming.

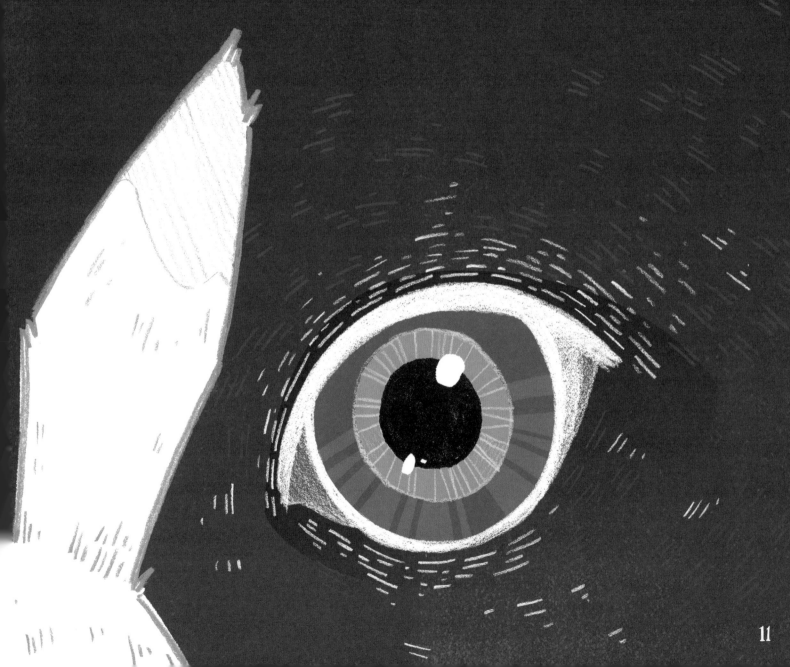

Again, Tiri called out, "Taaq, taaq, taaq," to make sure Ukaliq could not bring back the daylight. He followed his nose to where the smell was coming from—a secret stash of caribou meat, hidden by humans! The people had planned to eat that caribou meat during the long winter, but Tiri was about to ruin their plan.

He whispered, "Taaq," one more time, dug quietly into the ground, and found the meat. He began eating, grateful that the light was not blinding him.

Ukaliq had lost track of Tiri, so she carefully said, "Ubluq, ubluq, ubluq."

The sun came up and she saw Tiri down in the valley, pawing at something in the ground. As she watched, he grew tired and began digging a burrow in the snow to take a nap.

While Ukaliq kept her ears open, ready for when Tiri decided he had had enough sleep, she could see the humans waking up to find some of their hidden caribou meat gone. She watched them bury the rest even deeper.

"Ubluq, ubluq, ubluq," Ukaliq whispered, trying to give them more time. She kept her ears down so that she looked just like a ball of snow. The humans didn't know she was helping them. They didn't even know her words were powerful enough to help them.

"Taaq, taaq, taaq!" someone called in the distance. Ukaliq knew that Tiri had woken up.

The sun began to set, so the humans went back to their iglu to rest for the night.

Ukaliq kept her distance from Tiri, but she concentrated on the sounds he was making. She knew he was sniffing around the hidden meat, trying to find a way to dig in.

"Ubluq, ubluq, ubluq," Ukaliq said, trying to help the humans by bringing back the daylight.

As the sky grew brighter, Tiri looked for the hare, trotting up into the hills to find her. "We need to figure out a way for both of us to find food," he said.

"How about we take turns?" Ukaliq suggested.

They agreed that Tiri would go first. "Taaq, taaq, taaq!" he called.

He looked around and sniffed deeply to find food. Thanks to Ukaliq, the humans had hidden the caribou meat deep in the ground, so he looked for something else. He dug into the snow to see if he could smell a siksik, a ground squirrel, in its hole in the earth. But the siksik's hole was not in the spot he remembered seeing in the summer.

"Ubluq, ubluq, ubluq," Ukaliq said, impatient to have her turn.

"I haven't even found anything to eat yet!" Tiri called out, annoyed.

"I gave you a lot of time. Next time look faster." Ukaliq began eating her frozen cranberries.

"Taaq, taaq, taaq!" said Tiri. "You already know where your food is, so you can eat in the dark." He continued sniffing out the siksik.

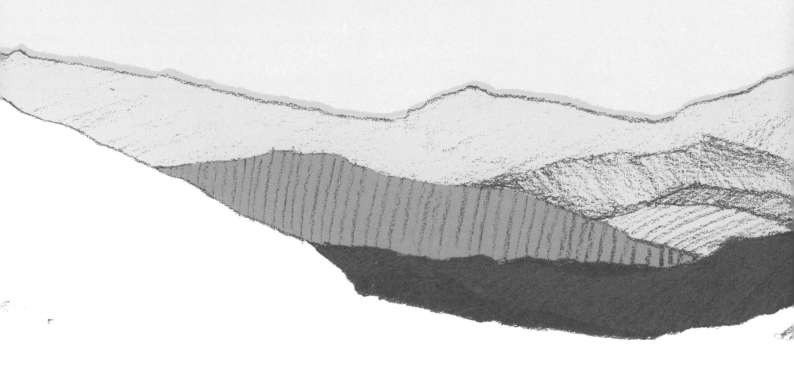

Ukaliq wondered if there was a way to make things fair.

"How about this: we give each other enough time to find a meal or two before the other changes the light in the sky," she suggested. "I'll give you more time if you will do the same for me."

The two agreed. And from then on Tiri had enough time to find a decent meal, and Ukaliq had enough time to find the plants she most liked to eat.

27

And so, Tiri and Ukaliq used the power of their words to bring the sun up into the sky and then to make it set. Taaq brought darkness and ubluq brought day.

Day came and replaced night, and when night had gone, day came again. This is why we now have day and night.

Paula Ikuutaq Rumbolt is from Baker Lake, Nunavut. She attended Concordia University in Montreal. Growing up, formal education was strongly encouraged by her grandmother, alongside traditional Inuit beliefs. After high school, Paula attended Nunavut Sivuniksavut in Ottawa. There she learned much about Inuit history and culture. She realized how important it is to connect with her culture and began to learn as much as she could after her year in the program. She is currently an elementary school Inuktitut teacher in Baker Lake and the co-owner of Hinaani Designs. Her first book for children was *The Legend of Lightning and Thunder*, which was shortlisted for the Canadian Library Association Book of the Year for Children.

Lenny Lishchenko is not a boy. She is an illustrator, graphic designer, and comics maker who will never give up the chance to draw a good birch tree. Ukrainian-born and Canadian-raised, she's interested in telling stories that people remember years later, in the early mornings, when everything is quiet and still. She's worked with clients such as Lenny Letter, Power Athletics Ltd., Alberta Venture, and Rubicon Publishing, and she is based out of Toronto, Ontario.

INHABIT
M E D I A
www.inhabitmedia.com